Care❤Bears™

Cheer Bear
and the TREASURE HUNT

Hodder
Children's
Books

We are the Care♥Bears™

Come and join us in Care-a-Lot...

I'm **Cheer.** I always look on the bright side!

I'm **Wonderheart,** I'm small, sweet and very curious.

I'm **Grumpy.** Inside, I'm really a big softie!

I'm **Tenderheart.** My
heart is in the right place.

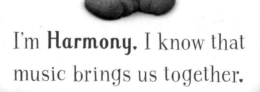

I'm **Harmony.** I know that
music brings us together.

I'm **Share.** I'm happiest
when I'm giving.

I'm **Funshine.** For me,
every day's a fun day.

It's the day of the Treasure
Hunt. Cheer Bear is
feeling happy.

"It's going to be so much
fun!" she calls to
Grumpy Bear.

"Fun is so annoying,"
Grumpy Bear mutters.

Tenderheart explains the rules. He is going to hide belly badges all around Care-a-Lot. The Care Bears must search in pairs and the team that finds the most badges will win a prize.

To make the hunt trickier no bear will be able to use their special powers.

How exciting! Wonderheart pulls the Care Bears' names out of a hat.

"Funshine Bear and Share Bear," she says.
"Harmony Bear and Surprise Bear and... oh my!
Cheer Bear must hunt with Grumpy Bear."

Cheer and Grumpy glare at each other.

"Can you try to be less cheerful?" grumbles Grumpy.

"Can you try to be less grumpy?" says Cheer.

The bears begin the
Treasure Hunt.

Harmony and Surprise
find the first belly badge.
They pull it out from
underneath a heavy rock.

Funshine and Share
find a badge in a tree.
They use a seesaw to
help them jump up
and reach it.

Everyone is working together nicely, apart from Cheer and Grumpy. They do not find ANY badges.

Tenderheart's belly
badge beacon lights
up in the sky. The
Treasure Hunt is over.
It is time to go back to
the Lighthouse.

Grumpy and Cheer are cross. Now they
will never win the special prize!

Wonderheart stands
outside the Lighthouse.
She holds up the Care
Crystal so that Tenderheart
can give the bears their
powers back.

Cheer and Grumpy stomp
back at just the wrong
moment. They bump
into Wonderheart...

...AND SHE DROPS THE CRYSTAL!

The crystal falls off the cloud, down towards Care-a-Lot.
Now the Care Bears can't get their powers back!

Cheer and Grumpy are both very sorry. They look everywhere for the Care Crystal.

"If only we had our bear powers," sighs Grumpy. "You could make a magic rainbow. The light would make the crystal sparkle so that we could spot it."

Suddenly, Cheer has an AMAZING idea.

"We don't need our powers!" she replies. "We just need teamwork."

The two bears work
together to pump water
from the stream up, up, up
into the air. The sun shines
and a real rainbow appears!

Something sparkles nearby.
It's the Care Crystal. Grumpy
and Cheer find it together.

"Good work, Grumpy,"
laughs Cheer.
"Give me a Care Hug!"

Back at the lighthouse, Tenderheart uses the Care Crystal
to give everyone's powers back.

Cheer and Grumpy are given something else, too.
They win a special prize for their great teamwork!

Tenderheart beams at Grumpy and Cheer.
"Your prize is to swap powers for one day!"

"Wow!" smiles Cheer.
"I can water my flowers
using your raincloud!"

Grumpy tries skating
on Cheer's rainbow.
"Woo hoo!" he cries.

Grumpy has changed
his mind. Fun is not so
annoying, after all!

"Have a rainbow-tastic day!"
laughs Cheer.